THE INNOCENT DAYS OF WAR

ALSO BY MARIO FORTUNATO

South

THE INNOCENT

DAYS OF WAR

MARIO FORTUNATO

Translated from the Italian by
Julia MacGibbon

OTHER PRESS | NEW YORK

Originally published in Italian as *I giorni innocenti della guerra* in 2007
by Bompiani, Firenze-Milano

This book was translated thanks to a grant awarded by
the Italian Ministry of Foreign Affairs and International Cooperation.

Production editor: Yvonne E. Cárdenas
Text designer: Patrice Sheridan
This book was set in Galliard and Birch by
Alpha Design & Composition of Pittsfield, NH

1 3 5 7 9 10 8 6 4 2

Library of Congress Cataloging-in-Publication Data
Names: Fortunato, Mario, author. | MacGibbon, Julia, translator.
Title: The innocent days of war / Mario Fortunato ; translated from the
Italian by Julia MacGibbon.
Other titles: Giorni innocenti della guerra. English
Description: New York : Other Press, 2025. | "Originally published in
Italian as I giorni innocenti della guerra in 2007 by Bompiani,
Firenze-Milano"—Title page verso.
Identifiers: LCCN 2025000234 (print) | LCCN 2025000235 (ebook) |
ISBN 9781635424140 (paperback) | ISBN 9781635424157 (ebook)
Subjects: LCSH: World War, 1939-1945—Italy—Fiction. | World War,
1939-1945—England—Fiction. | LCGFT: War fiction. | Novels.
Classification: LCC PQ4866.O74 G5613 2025 (print) |
LCC PQ4866.O74 (ebook) | DDC 853/.914—dc23/eng/20250226
LC record available at https://lccn.loc.gov/2025000234
LC ebook record available at https://lccn.loc.gov/2025000235

In memory of Elena de Angeli

.

1

STEFANO PORTELLI WOULD REMEMBER THAT VIR-
ginal, never-ending kiss for a very long time. He
would remember the smell of wet earth and the im-
mense silence all around, a silence broken only by the
rapid thudding of the blood in their veins. He would
remember the treetops moving slowly in the distance,
and his own body flooding with a sudden drowsiness.
That, above all. He will never forget it, the very sudden
longing to sleep, and then, instead, running away, running back to the house, away from his wife, away from
everything. Over time, that kiss will become familiar
but unapproachable terrain: a mountain on the horizon
buried in his heart.

He had met Eleonora Polidori at a party. He was born
in 1912, she in '16. A yearlong engagement and then
the wedding. At which point, Stefano was fresh out of

law school. Law, like his father and his grandfather. He can't claim to be brilliant, but he is a serious and resolute young man. Law, as Stefano sees it, is not empty, artificial rhetoric; it doesn't mean knowing how to erect a tower of words, interpretations, or hypotheses over a void. For Stefano, justice has concrete, constructive foundations. It is a way of thinking, or an ideal, that is poured into everyday actions, into the honest toil of daily life. In his youthful imaginings, studying law represents the first step toward becoming a decent man, a just man, who will judge and defend his own actions and those of others.

Eleonora's story is different. She reads lots of novels and loves poetry. No regular, formal schooling. In the tiny villages of northern Lazio like the one where she lives, school and (in the best of cases) university are reserved for boys. Her family owns a little land. Her father could almost be described as a peasant farmer. Her two brothers—Ernesto and Giuseppe—are noisy and glib, and enthusiastic fans of the Fascist regime. Eleonora is unassuming by nature. Very reserved. When she realizes that Stefano is courting her, she feigns a certain disinterest. But it's not genuine. She likes that young man who is not much older than she is and who inspires her with a sense of quiet satisfaction. She approves of Stefano's kind, discreet ways. She likes his blandly Socialist ideals. Eleonora has not had a regular, formal education, but she has always harbored a certain regard for the idea of culture—a word she thinks of not as meaning something precise but as a kind of tuning fork, vibrating and emitting concentric circles of sound. In her eyes, Stefano is in every sense a cultured man: He comes from a family of professionals; he is about to graduate in law. And once Fascism comes to an end (Eleonora is sincerely convinced of the fact: Fascism will come to an end), she is certain he will have a role to play in the new political order.

But at the party, when the two of them meet, there is no time for considerations such as these. The first time they meet, simpler things take precedence. A glance, a gesture made by a pair of hands, the cut of his suit. Who knows why that particular glance, that gesture, and the cut of that suit imprint themselves in a way that will later be hard to forget. Eleonora and Stefano are, both of them, levelheaded young people. No sentimental hyperbole. He asks if he can see her again; she accepts. She does so with a hint of coolness, not because she wants to give herself airs but to put Stefano to the test. If something is to come of this, she would like it to be serious, she thinks.

The party doesn't go on until late: It is the end of May; the evenings are still cool. 1938. Rome is only thirty miles away yet might as well be another planet. The rest of the world is very remote. Maybe there will be a war, but not now, not yet. Right now, they look out at the view from the terrace, the young men drink wine, and a few people dance under the vigilant gazes of family members.

That evening, at any rate, there is no kiss.

Stefano reads only law books. Even after completing his university studies, even when he is no longer working at the Police Court (he never will be a practicing attorney—at the end of the day too one-sided, too insubstantial a profession to satisfy the instincts that make of him a natural-born legal philologist) he will carry on devouring legal texts. They are his great passion, his great pride. Among other things, he dreams of putting together the largest library in the area. Something to hand down, one day, to future generations, so that his name might be remembered as that of a man whose life—every second of it—honored the concept, the very notion, of justice.

This veritable obsession is not universally appreciated. In Stefano's disquisitions on the Code of Justinian or the Napoleonic Code or the principles of common law, local party officials note a subtle criticism of the regime. Even his father has words to say with regard to those monothematic interests of his. Eleonora, on the other hand, will come to love their subtlety and his prodigious erudition.

Sadly, the conversations they have will not last long. Conversations which, if we are to be entirely honest, are monologues recited by him, with rare interruptions on her part to ask a few timid questions. Conversations regarding the Napoleonic Code or the principles of common law. The marriage will last only two years. Two full and authentically happy years.

About which there is not much to say. There never is when everything goes well and concord reigns. To which we might add, happiness is always too fleeting to leave any time for detailed descriptions.

War breaks out for real. To begin with, nobody notices. It feels like an abstract concept, an implausible claim only registered by folk who happen to make the journey from the village to Rome and perhaps read the newspapers—an irrelevant number of individuals. When even the local boys start leaving for the front, that's when the war becomes real.

No one seriously understands the ins and outs of the compulsory draft. In Eleonora's family, the eldest son, Ernesto, who is twenty-seven, volunteers for service. He adores Il Duce and is a snappy dresser: The uniform undeniably suits him. He thinks of the war as a sort of catwalk. Her other brother, Giuseppe, is champing at the bit, longing to follow in Ernesto's footsteps. He expects to be called up soon. Stefano, meanwhile, is more than happy to remain at home. He has been married to Eleonora for just a few months. The two of them consider themselves very lucky, and in effect they are. As if the world were unchanged, he still has his job at the

Police Court, and he manages the property (not a great deal of it—mostly planted with olive trees) that his wife has brought as her dowry, while she devotes herself to the home. They also consider themselves lucky because all the chatter floating around has nothing to do with them personally. How could ridiculous claims to far-away lands have anything to do with them? And all the talk of imperial pasts and military glories and virtues? Why should they pay any attention to the risible, offensive rhetoric that animates the buildup to all wars? As a matter of fact, Stefano nurses dreams of global peace and justice, dreams in which a supranational organization regulates and defuses eventual conflicts or—and preferably—disagreements between nations. And does so on the basis of an unambiguous charter, a governing code that will be universal, and in its own way mathematical . . .

Luckily, in those first months of war there are no local deaths to mourn. Eleonora and Stefano know no young men who have died in combat. They hear news of a few acquaintances being wounded, but nothing tragic or irreparable.

Despite the war being a distant but—they imagine— painful and horrible thing, both begin to think they might want a child. They talk about it for the first time toward the end of autumn in 1940. Italy has just launched hostilities against Greece; Adelchi Serena has been acclaimed secretary of the National Fascist Party; the Racial Laws have already demonstrated what stuff their fellow Italians are made of. It all seems so sense-less. Eleonora and Stefano are, after a fashion, con-scious of that, but they don't lose heart. Although, to tell the truth, Stefano had been thinking of leaving his job at the Police Court. Eleonora has dissuaded him, and yes, for motives that are also financial but above all out of a conviction that he is as well-equipped as anyone to make a quiet, stubborn stand against the folly that seems to be engulfing everything.

And so the two of them talk about having a baby, one evening when the air is so balmy and soft that it seems impossible winter should ever arrive. They are out on the little terrace, at home after supper. A few clouds drift by. Mount Soratte is mutely bright in the moonlight. Now more than ever, its silhouette brings to mind a giant's face—a supine giant who has aban-doned himself to sleep.

Sex has never been something much discussed by the two of them. Stefano is a straitlaced man. He does not belong to that class of men for whom a woman's body is a refuge to be made use of as and when desired. He respects his wife's rhythms, her silences. Which is why Eleonora has never once felt threatened by him, and why she is able to love him the way one loves a landscape.

A handful of words: What will the baby be like? Boy or girl? One kiss. Followed by others.

2

TWO YEARS GO QUICKLY BY. IN APRIL 1941, ELEONORA Polidori is a young woman expecting her first child. She is often confined to her bed. Her mother and her younger sister, Nina, help with the household chores. The family doctor doesn't say anything out of the ordinary. He says she needs to be patient, that there's only one cure for this, and that cure is known as rest. Eleonora doesn't fret. Staying in bed and daydreaming is not unpleasant. It's a luxury she has never been able to permit herself. She takes the whole thing as a sort of forced holiday. Stefano, on the other hand, seems to be worried. He explains that it's because of the international situation: The English have just given the Italian fleet a pounding at Cape Matapan, although the regime is apparently still firmly on its feet, and now there's talk of war with the Soviet Union. Even locally, a few deaths start being recorded.

Ernesto writes his sister hotly patriotic letters. He is writing from Cyrenaica, in eastern Libya; he is a member of the troops under the sole command of Field Marshal Rommel. Ernesto is proud of what he is doing; he says he feels part of an elect band. He talks at length and not infrequently about the importance the German comrades place, even during combat, on keeping their uniforms immaculate. Their brother, Giuseppe, who is four years younger, reads Ernesto's letters impatiently. He is still at home in the village and itching to leave for the eastern front: What's keeping them from calling him up?

But it is not this that worries Stefano. He is worried about his wife who, beneath the bedsheets, looks increasingly wan. He fears for that first child of theirs who seems not to want to come into this world and is causing all sorts of problems. Every evening, after supper, Stefano shuts himself into his study for an hour. The law books he reads are of great consolation. What he finds there, inside them, is the fairness, the justice, the orderliness that the world appears to have mislaid—who knows where and who knows how? It is only there, in the pages of his favorite texts, that Stefano finds the courage he needs to keep going in a here and now he has come to find utterly ghastly.

Having read for an hour, he pokes his head into their bedroom and invariably guesses that Eleonora is sleeping. He takes his shoes off and wriggles carefully out of his jacket. His silhouette forms the hesitant, slightly rounded movements of someone who is trying to make no noise. She watches him with a tenderness that has something childlike to it. Her feelings toward him aren't maternal; she is not one of those women who love their men the way one loves a little child. If anything, it is she who feels like a girl—and Stefano is her playmate. Therefore, whenever he enters the shadowy fug of their room, taking care to do so unobtrusively, moving as softly as a cat, she always finds herself wanting to play hide-and-seek, or one of those games where you close your eyes, and the minute you do so, as if by magic, you become invisible and—just like that!—the rest of the world disappears.

Instead, they usually talk. Stefano tells her about whatever it is he has just been reading, or what his thoughts on it are, at any rate, and she is genuinely interested, as is clear from the number of questions she asks—questions that are never perfunctory. They also talk about the war, about Mussolini and Hitler, for whom they nurse a contempt that's all the stronger because by day it remains unvoiced. Every evening they talk through the day's events: the news from the front; the letters from Ernesto (he has been promoted to corporal); Nina, who didn't come around today. Because she has the flu. And at the Police Court? Oh, at the Police Court there's nothing much going on; the law, as such, no longer exists: There's only violence now, just violence. You mustn't say that, don't let them hear you saying that; it's already a miracle you haven't been called up. Yes, but for what it's worth...

They talk and talk. And, as can be the case for people who share bonds of intimacy that aren't expressed in words, they talk and often don't actually say very much—nothing worth remembering. The baby is due in July. But he is never mentioned.

Little by little, as the pregnancy progresses, Eleonora feels increasingly detached. All that daydreaming done while stuck in bed leaves her with a mental fogginess, a confusion she doesn't know how to clear up. Bit by bit, the threads of her arguments get lost in the void. Stefano is the first to notice. He discusses it with her doctor who, however, dismisses it as nothing much. As doctors do.

Eleonora begins to have neither opinions nor points of view. She, who has always been a thoughtful and sometimes pedantic interlocutor, is now simply silent. There is an empty space inside her, and she has no idea how it got there.

The days drift by slowly and vaguely. Stefano's thoughts grow as mazy as tangled threads. The first hot days of the summer. It's clear, now, that Germany is going to invade the Soviet Union. Giuseppe, who often states the obvious, can't stop repeating it: The Soviet Union has to be invaded and Communism has to be stamped out. They need to get a move on. Right now. Get to Moscow and kill Stalin. He, Giuseppe, is ready to go.

One evening, a little earlier than usual, Stefano enters the room his wife has been lying in for weeks now. He persuades her to get up from the bed. A few paces, just as far as the little terrace, so that she can enjoy the fresh air for a bit. To begin with, Eleonora doesn't want to, she's too tired; then she comes around to the idea. She's grateful her husband suggested it. She looks out at the silvery olive trees, at that endless sky she would like to melt away into, and in her mind all of it bleaches itself of color, as if nothing in life has ever existed, as if it has all been a dream or a fairy tale.

When she loses the baby, Eleonora is lost. She dies early in the morning, with a single sudden and definitive moan. The house fills with whispers, sobs, closed doors.

The first thought that crosses Stefano's mind is connected with their wedding day. He remembers having been happy. So happy that he felt almost punch-drunk. He remembers an enormous number of happy thoughts surging through him and, it seemed at the time, overwhelming him. Even the others, standing there next to him, had seemed suddenly to want to be happy. Where is it now, all that happiness?

3

IN 1941, NINA IS JUST FOURTEEN YEARS OLD. SHE IS very different from her older sister. Petite and as light as a butterfly, she often laughs for no particular reason. She likes walking—even, occasionally, off into the open countryside. Like Eleonora, and thanks to Eleonora—who treated her like a daughter—she has learned to read and write despite not having been to school. Nina doesn't care about the war, about Fascism and all those complicated words she hears being pronounced when her brothers are talking, or when it's her brother-in-law, Stefano Portelli, who's speaking. She just wants to be able to wander off, slipping out from under her mother's thumb, stopping to gossip with people here and there. She walks along with her chin held high, rather boldly, and all kinds of thoughts bloom in her mind and fill her with a puppyish excitement.

The day Eleonora's life ended was, for Nina, a silent, bewildering day. In all her young life, no one had ever died: She hadn't known her grandparents, except as photographs hanging in the kitchen. Every now and then someone in the village passed away, but they weren't friends or relatives. The death of her sister opened a dark, sticky breach in her mind—a wound that would ache on many occasions. She didn't feel sad for her brother-in-law, or for the baby who would have been her nephew: She felt sad for herself. Nina had lost not just the companion of her childhood games but the one person in the family she thought of as having anything to teach her, a sister who was something of a mother figure, and above all a young woman who, despite being very unlike her, in Nina's eyes embodied the very ideal of womanhood. Without Eleonora there, who was going to teach her the secrets of love?

For many days afterward, Stefano Portelli felt as lifeless as a clod of earth. When evening came and he shut himself into his study, which now seemed small and empty, he clung to the books that crammed his desk and the shelves. A man lost at sea. Or a man on the run.

He would shut the door into the room and, for a second, savor the balm of darkness. A few paces forward, habitual gestures. Once the light was switched on, the perfect little world of his books reappeared exactly as it always had been. Sitting down, he flicked through a volume chosen at random. Only his hands moved, but he didn't notice that. He couldn't focus on the open pages; his attention was caught by little, insignificant things: that ribbon of light on the floor, a dirty glass, the butt of a spent cigarette. His thoughts drifted from one thing to another somewhere outside his head, and they were wrapped in a nocturnal haze.

The war and politics and Hitler and Mussolini no longer meant anything. The world had receded into the distance all of a sudden.

He walked out of the study. Time to rest. Or try, at least. But how could he sleep in that bed where Eleonora had abandoned him? In the half darkness, without switching the light on, he pushed open the doors leading onto the terrace, and Mount Soratte's outline entered the room. The surrounding hills loomed blackly, almost as if they were screening something mysterious and terrible. Each and every evening, he took a pillow off the bed, slid the chaise longue all the way over to the open terrace doors, and lay down. His mind was an empty space. Barnlike. The odd thought fluttered around in there—unfamiliar thoughts, long as shadows. Then, finally, he fell asleep.

Now, even Giuseppe had gone off to war. Toward the end of June 1941, Mussolini had, like Germany and Finland, sent a contingent into the Soviet Union. So Giuseppe's call to arms had not been long coming. With the slightly ominous ebullience typical of younger siblings, the boy had set off on the long journey that would take him into the much-despised Russia. The local villages were emptying out: Stefano thought of himself as a surviving relic—the one, timorous representative of a now forgotten species. And while, from the African front, Ernesto continued writing excited letters, befuddling the family with all the exotic names of the places he sent news from, almost from the get-go they heard nothing from Giuseppe—the odd letter during his training period in northern Italy, and then a lengthy silence. The young man had, it seemed, been swallowed up by that Communist world he so wanted to defeat. Months went by. No news. His parents tried asking. They went to Rome, to the Ministry of War. They begged. From time to time his mother found herself picturing that unlucky, headstrong boy of hers, lost amid the ice of some small Soviet town. Who knows if it was true that the folk there ate human beings?

By Christmas 1941, Germany and Italy were also at war with the United States. Nina and Stefano were all that was left of the younger generation. It was a sad little Christmas, rapidly over and dominated by quarrels and confabulations. They had to do with property. The olive grove that Eleonora had been given as her dowry now belonged to Stefano. Deprived of both sons, the Polidori family was struggling to get by. In addition to which, there was Nina. Sooner or later, she would want to marry. What dowry could she possibly take with her? Bedsheets, towels, tablecloths, and lengths of Flanders linen, her mother carefully calculated. Their savings, however, barely stretched to surviving the so-called wartime economy. A vineyard had already been sold. Their situation was looking more critical than the gloomiest of forecasts. Stefano offered to hand back the olive grove. He was a single man with a job that remained secure; he could cope without the income from a thing that, ultimately, wasn't really his. Eleonora's parents refused: It would have caused a minor scandal in the village. What would people have said? That they were so poverty-stricken they had asked their son-in-law to give back the dowry he had legitimately inherited from his late wife? No. Nothing doing.

In early January, Ernesto came home on leave. He immediately proposed an alternative solution. A solution that would remedy more than one problem. He mentioned it hesitantly to begin with, and then with the assertive, energetic self-assurance of the military strategist he fancied himself to be. It involved Nina. Or rather: Stefano and Nina. Together.

Ernesto was the same as ever—vain and dapper. The nasty wound on his left foot, the wound that was taking so long to heal, seemed almost not to concern him. During the visits he paid to relatives and neighbors, he continually apologized for the state of his uniform. He remained at home for just a few weeks, eager to get back to fighting in an Africa he had already fallen in love with.

There were many discussions, and even rows, over the course of the days Ernesto spent at home. In

Germany, the regime's assembled upper echelons were at that very moment mandating the extermination of the Jews. That fact was still a secret, but in Stefano's eyes the anti-Jewish laws and edicts were enough in and of themselves to be definitive proof of Nazism's grim bestiality. Ernesto, on the other hand, shrugged off the initial persecution of Germany's Jewry. Sometimes he blamed all the Communist propaganda, but he also blamed the Jewish lobby who monopolized the world of finance and the press. The result was endless bickering, which left Nina speechless with dismay. Were her brother, their brother-in-law, and half the world's population really coming to blows over arguments that just went in circles? Had it really not occurred to any of them that nothing mattered more than love?

They just had to hope the English and Americans would get here soon, said Stefano. That was the only way they'd ever be free of all this barbarity. He had always been an admirer of Anglo-Saxon manners, and therefore imagined the landing—of the British troops in particular—being a calm and orderly affair, rigorously respecting the rules not just of warfare but also of decorum. England was the land of five meals a day, a peerless example of affluence and efficiency.

4

AT TWENTY-ONE YEARS OF AGE, ALASTAIR ORMISTON is one of those young Englishmen who seem born to spend their lives going from one picnic or shoot to the next, destined to live in beautiful homes with servants and bunches of flowers all over the place. He has not followed in his father's footsteps. Dr. Ormiston is one of London's most highly regarded specialists in internal medicine; his Harley Street rooms are frequented by numerous members of Parliament. Alastair has preferred to study the arts. Like other young men of his generation, he dreamed of going off to fight in Spain— for freedom. He couldn't. The family wouldn't allow it: too young. Given which, he has instead worshipped Wystan Auden, who has written some wonderful lines on the theme of the Spanish civil war.

Secretly, Alastair wants to be a poet. Although he has never yet composed a poem, he imagines them all the time. He makes mental notes in the most improbable of places and at the oddest of moments—on the London Underground or when he's having a bath. He writes and rewrites, corrects and alters and chisels away: All of it's kept in his head. Alastair is no fan of vacuous improvisation, pointlessly free verse, or simple outpourings of emotion. Poetry, he thinks, is never a personal thing but quite the contrary: a sublime application of intelligence; a way of reintroducing order and measuredness into a chaotic world. Auden and T. S. Eliot are his idols. In their work, he finds a balance he craves and has lost. One day—he tells himself every so often—he will succeed in transferring onto the written page all those myriad words, rhymes, pauses, and tercets composed so painstakingly over the years. For now, there is just one small, khaki-green notebook, held together with a band of black elastic, which never leaves his side. No poems in it, though: It contains the sometimes rather dull, insignificant diary of a life measured out with lunches and weekends in the country. Which, for precisely that reason, feels to him like a dull and insignificant sort of life.

The truth is, having graduated from university, Alastair doesn't really know what to do with himself. The society girls in London bore him to death, and so do the chaps. Only Edna could ever convince him to change his ways and stop dithering. But Edna's like him: She wants no truck with convention; she wants unalloyed freedom, and ideally a place somewhere a long way from home where it's possible to live as one chooses. They really are far too alike, Edna and he, to ever end up in bed together. At Cambridge they were known as the Siamese twins—to which crueler tongues added, "Guess which one of the two is the male." And now Edna has made her mind up. She has volunteered as a nurse. Over the telephone she said, "Think of all the gorgeous naked boys I'll get my hands on."

"Oh, she'll have her wicked way with all of them," he'd thought with a prick of the childish envy he doesn't know how to suppress.

Physically they differ. Edna is not tall. She has black hair and dark, sharp eyes, and a mole on her right cheek that gives her an eighteenth-century look: She could easily be Spanish, or maybe Jewish. She has a loud laugh, and people generally describe her as volcanic. Alastair, on the other hand, is rather tall and lanky, with very pale eyes and skin. Almost blond. One hundred percent so in the summer months. He thinks of himself as a melancholy type, and at parties or fashionable events he does effectively come across that way, but he is also equipped with a particularly wicked sense of humor, which is what has drawn them to each other from the minute they met. Both love Auden and literature in general, although Edna nurses no creative ambitions: Poetry, for her, is something to be discussed incessantly, endlessly interpreted, and sometimes even ridiculed. Both of them detest traditional novels and fashionable authors like Somerset Maugham. As far as they are concerned, only E. M. Forster counts for anything, or the Bloomsbury group (so wonderfully effete).

Alastair has met Mr. and Mrs. Woolf. In October 1939. But since this was at a very formal dinner party, he hadn't managed to utter a word. From time to time, Virginia had looked at him with interest from the other side of the table; then at one point he had decided it wasn't him she was looking at but the girl sitting next to him, the daughter of the house, young Priscilla Kaye, who was the same age as Alastair (and insufferable). But no, it had been him she was staring at.

There have been a few military Ormistons. Not very many, to tell the truth: Alastair's family has solid upper-middle-class and mercantile roots. All the same, the odd officer or two has cropped up. Added to which, the war now being fought across Europe is really just an expanded version of the Spanish conflict. A blown-up version—for lack of a better term. The enemy is the same: dictatorship and Fascism. The Germans and Italians have to be stopped, without question, even at the cost of engaging in alliances that would have been unthinkable just yesterday. Alastair would be prepared to take orders from some idiot conservative colonel, for the sake of fighting the Nazis' barbarism. He too will volunteer. He spends an entire night mulling it over, a night during which he reads and rereads favorite bits of Shakespeare, and continually wonders whether or not he'll come to regret this decision. He also asks himself if it mightn't be nobler to do as his beloved Auden has done and espouse a radical pacifism. In the morning, Alastair telephones Edna. She answers in a voice thick with sleep. For no one else would she ever drag herself out of bed this early, but for Alastair she makes an exception—the umpteenth. Her tone is, in any case, testy. He huffs and sighs into the mouthpiece. Edna says, "Darling, can't you use human language like the rest of us?" Alastair huffs and sighs all over again. He says, "I've made up my mind. I'm going to volunteer right away, like you." And he adds, "Think of all the naked chaps I'll get to see in the showers."

"Yes, but you won't have your wicked way with any of them."

"Cow."

It is early 1940 and the war could still be mistaken for an honorable thing. The air echoes with notions such as "appeasement" and "gentlemen's agreement." Military service has just been made obligatory: Alastair shouldn't have long to wait for his call-up papers. In any case, he's volunteering. That's settled. The government has just fallen and Chamberlain is about to be replaced by Winston Churchill—who is, it's true, another Conservative, but at least not set on reducing himself to making pacts with the revolting regimes in Germany and Italy. In the family, no one makes any fuss about Alastair's plan. Dr. Ormiston and his wife think their son would have been called up anyway; they might as well take his martial zeal to be a sign of something positive. The boy had also wanted to go off to Spain as a volunteer a few years back but was too young for it at the time; that he should be charting his own course now is no bad thing. Who knows? Perhaps he has taken after his uncle, Arthur Bradshaw, captain of a Royal Navy schooner?

Alastair makes a beeline for the RAF. He rightly imagines that the fact he speaks French and a fair amount of Italian (learned from the librettos of the operas of his beloved Puccini and Leoncavallo) will prove to be a useful calling card. He doesn't give a moment's thought to the hard training, the exhausting physical exercises, and the trials he will undergo in order to keep the most basic of feelings under control—fear, for example, and instincts as primitive as terror of the void. Incredibly, Alastair overcomes all these obstacles with relative ease. The six weeks of training at Shinfield Park go by in a flash. The young man discovers that, far from being a form of torture, aviation's steely discipline is actually a form of liberation—liberation, first and foremost, from himself. Alastair comes to see that obeying orders, keeping to a meticulously programmed daily schedule, never having a free moment if not the time it takes, in the evening, to read a few pages of a book—all of this, he comes to realize—shelters him from his own most secret demons, providing him with a code of conduct that is impersonal and dispassionate, and guarantees not only greater efficiency but above all an unexpected serenity: a state of detachment; a state of grace that people in the Far East would call *satori*.

He gets regular letters from Edna, who has been seconded to a hospital in Wales, where she too is undergoing training. The letters are invariably very jolly. Edna talks about cases of diphtheria and pulmonary infections as if they were garden parties or afternoon teas. She describes the Welsh as being quite mad, and predictably enough, she already knows everything there is to know about nursing. She could just as easily have studied medicine as English literature; it wouldn't have made much difference. Alastair always replies with alacrity. He writes his letters in the evening, in his bunk, sacrificing that day's ration of reading. He doesn't, however, succeed in giving a tone of breezy vagueness to the things he writes. He would like to: More often than not he finds himself aping his friend's style, but it doesn't work. The impersonality, the detachment that in daylight hours lend his demeanor such self-assurance are transformed into a foggy mental opacity by the act of putting pen to paper. Alastair feels heavy. As though his body were waterlogged. As though it were bloated and obtuse.

Having finished his training, he comes back to London on leave. The city seems frivolous now, and irresponsible. He goes to the theater but doesn't much enjoy it. He meets up with a few old friends; he strolls through the streets of Mayfair. Overcome with boredom and a strange anxiety, he finds himself wanting to go straight back to RAF headquarters. Perhaps because Edna's not around? One thing's for certain: London has grown foreign to him. The city even feels slightly menacing. He is constantly in doubt as to how to behave or what to say. One afternoon, making his way home, at the corner of Piccadilly where Green Park begins, Alastair locks eyes with another military man. Army, not air force. He has the florid complexion of a country lad, big hands, a thickset, muscular body. The young man makes a barely perceptible gesture the meaning of which isn't clear. A vague greeting? Or an invitation to follow him? Just enough for Alastair to feel his heart flip wildly in his chest.

Get away from here. This evening. Out of harm's way. That's imperative now.

At home, the decision surprises no one. It has simply come slightly earlier than expected. Dr. and Mrs. Ormiston choose to read it as a sign of normal youthful intemperance. No one else in the family even notices: They are all inured to the eccentricities of the older brother they call "the Red" on account of his political beliefs.

In just over an hour, Alastair is at Paddington Station. Once he gets to Reading, it will take him very little time to reach the RAF's headquarters at Shinfield Park. It is late evening when, from the open window of the railway car he's traveling in, he smells the countryside's characteristic aroma in the air—that blend of earth and dung that, perhaps because he has, among other things, recently been reading Freud, whisks him back to the developmental stage in which an infant recognizes himself by the odor of his own feces. A point at which none of us yet knows what secrets are.

5

NINA AND POOR ELEONORA HAD A SECRET—A SECRET
that will never be revealed. The young woman had con-
fided in her older sister not long before she died. It's
something that racks Nina's conscience. Surprisingly,
Eleonora's advice wasn't to tell the parish priest or their
parents all about it. She simply said it would be better
not to talk about it. Better to forgive and forget. As time
goes by, she added, it won't be hard to forgive or forget.

Nina, however, will think about that secret on many
occasions. It's true, as time goes by she does forgive,
but she never will manage to forget. She will never forget it.

Sergio lives just steps away from their house. He's tall;
his eyes are a brindled green. Dark hair, hands like vices.
When he plays games, the animal energy he puts into
it frightens his companions. Naturally, of all the young

men in the village, he is—he claims—the top dog; he's the best. He flaunts his pride. He flaunts his muscular physique. He flaunts everything about himself. If ever he smiles, Nina feels like she's turning to stone. She feels as if her body were turning, all of a sudden, into a branch of coral. Deep underwater. At the bottom of the sea.

There is an age gap of a year between Sergio and Nina. Just a year. Just enough for Sergio to claim that ascendency too. He says that for some time now he has had a passionate lover—an older, married woman who adores him and would do anything he asks. Nina doesn't believe it; she doesn't want to believe it. She would never admit as much, but she is jealous of Sergio's secret lover, whom she sometimes imagines being a sweet figure, like Eleonora. But something doesn't add up: In Eleonora she sees none of the wildness that Sergio describes when he tells her about the other woman. Could it be that her sister is a woman devoid of that attribute—apparently so important where men are concerned?

Nina comes up with no answers. As far as she can see, Sergio is a champion at a kind of virility that, as of yet, means very little to her. Apart from turning to stone in front of a smile. She is engaged in a teasing and brazen sort of competition with him: Whatever the young man says, Nina questions, downplays, or even ridicules. And so, between the two of them, a blind, stubborn contest has begun, a battle in which each vies to demonstrate their superiority.

Sergio has frequently mentioned his mysterious lover. He describes her as a thirty-year-old with a thick chestnut mane, beautiful breasts, a generous sensuality. In the young man's accounts, everything about the woman sounds lavish and overabundant, as though her body were the consequence of an ethical principle. The woman is married but, as luck would have it, her husband is far away—whether off at war or busy elsewhere is not clear, and at the end of the day it doesn't matter. In the overall economy of the tales Sergio spins, the figure of his rival barely features—a rough outline, void of character and nuance. But since Nina continues to believe him only in part, and indeed often adopts an attitude so skeptical that it wounds his pride, he proposes a bet. He will take his secret lover out to a particular spot in the countryside. Nina will be hiding a few paces away, so that she can watch without being seen. In exchange, though, the following day she will have to swim naked in the Tiber with Sergio. In a voice that sounds hesitant because she is trembling, Nina agrees. She demands only that, should the young man's boasts turn out to have been true and should she therefore have to swim naked in the river, he limit himself to watching her from a distance. Sergio nods. All right.

The color is leaching out of the day. The clearing overlooked by Mount Soratte seems made of some lilac-colored substance, amid which the trees—what few trees there are—look very still and aloof, while the light overhead flickers and drifts between their branches as though following a pattern of its own invention, a shape that refuses to form. A trace of the day remains— a residual pause. Nina is crouching behind a bush that gives off an unpleasant smell of rotting vegetation. All of a sudden, coming from the trees in the distance, she hears what might be the buzz of voices. Then silence, and then the noise of footsteps in the grass. Nina half closes her eyes. If that is Sergio, he will make his way to the spot they've agreed on, not ten paces away.

It is Sergio, and there is somebody with him. A flowery dress. The couple embraces and then moves apart. The young man gestures: He's showing the woman something, and for a second Nina fears it might be her he's pointing to. She's afraid it might all be a prank, a joke at her expense. Sergio looks rugged. He looks feral. The woman—who, in effect, could be around thirty and does boast a fine mane of hair—kneels down in front of him and starts to stroke his groin. They are very close by. Nina hears, or thinks she hears, the couple's labored breathing. Or perhaps this is the sound of her own breathing. She shuts her eyes for a moment. When she reopens them, Sergio is naked from the waist down and is rubbing his sex across the woman's face and into her mouth, and is looking in Nina's direction with an air of malice. Nina instantly feels humiliated. Sergio is a real man, powerful, arrogantly powerful, while she is simply a fool. And now the couple has rolled to the ground. Nina wants to get away from here, the lesson has sufficed, and yet she would also like to stay exactly where she is and spy on them, and she wonders if she, too, will one day find herself doing the same things the woman is now doing. All that sensuality disgusts her. Above all, she—the woman—disgusts her. For him, though, she feels a submissive sort of admiration. For the thing he embodies.

Nina has no idea how long this scene goes on. She will remember him glancing repeatedly in her direction—the pointedness of it, the way he stares directly at her, is something she will not forget—and she will remember the impression made on her by the sight of that fluid suddenly spurting from Sergio's sex. The woman's body is a cloud, blurred and indistinct. Which is also the way Nina feels. Does she have it in her to take her clothes off in front of him tomorrow?

But the following day Sergio doesn't turn up for their rendezvous. Nina arrives punctually. She is sweating heavily but still hopes she looks confident. In a show put on chiefly for her own benefit, her movements are dignified and coquettish. As the minutes tick by and she doesn't see him arrive, her composure crumbles. She isn't sure what to do. She decides to remain where she is for a little while longer. She will wait for half an hour. But there's no sign of Sergio. There isn't a single noise to be heard. The river flows softly and disinterestedly by. The afternoon melts away. Like an unspoken truth, the sunset lasts for a very long time. Before she makes up her mind to go home, Nina slowly undresses. Off comes her skirt, off comes her muslin blouse, off comes each sandal and everything else. Naked and silent, just like the water she is lowering herself into, Nina suddenly senses that she is not alone. Shivering as it comes into contact with the dark liquid the river is made of, her still-girlish body seems to flicker and sway. A few yards away, invisible and all-seeing, Sergio's eyes follow her movements as if he were a believer and this were a religious procession. The young man whispers, but she can't hear him. He repeats the same words to himself, over and over again. He wants Nina to kiss him. Just once, just one kiss, one kiss, one kiss. A kiss on the mouth.

6

London, September 20, 1940

My Darling Alastair,
It feels like a hundred years: We haven't seen each
other for a hundred years. You must be a new person,
with all those naked chaps milling round you in the
showers and the dorms. I'm not. Or rather, yes, I am
different. But not because of spending weeks with those
raving lunatics in Wales. I've been a different person
since I got back to London. In Wales all we had to deal
with was tummy trouble and pneumonia—nothing
terribly exciting. In the evening I used to go out with
other girls from the course. We had a laugh and told
each other silly gossip—Jane's in love with George.
Uh-oh! But did you know Matron's having it off with
Dr. Robey?—silly things like that. And it was fine,
everyone was happy. I never said a word about having

studied at Cambridge. Perish the thought. They'd have been scandalized. They'd have written me off as a bluestocking and I'd have wound up spending my evenings alone, like a pathetic fool.

It was when I got back here that something snapped. Isn't it a shame we didn't get a chance to see each other, though? Your mother tells me you went back before your leave was up, and by now I expect you'll have left Shinfield Park and must be at the base in Doncaster. I'm at the Royal Hospital. It's only been a little while, but it's already hellish. No more tummy aches and pneumonias, no mothers being demanding and children being capricious. The problems are of a different order. Arms and legs detached from bodies, cracked skulls and brains dripping onto the floor, and screams and moans and a constant stench of death that never leaves you, not even when you get home. It's always there in your nostrils, as if there's something burning all the time inside you and around you, and you yourself are somehow the root of it.

You are often on my mind. My Alastair. Dear old Alastair, I've grown so old in the space of just a few weeks. Every day I'm terrified I'll go back into the hospital and, in the middle all those poor mangled bodies coming back from the front, there you'll be, unrecognizable and silent. And so I roam the wards like a madwoman, counting the dead and the wounded and almost screaming with joy when I don't see you there in among them.

I've started to pray. Yes, me. Praying. I'm not quite sure what the devil it is I'm praying for or who it is I'm praying to. I pray it'll all end. I pray under the blankets, at night. Have you ever prayed, Alastair? Have you ever prayed and not even known what it is you're praying for? I suppose it's fear that impels one to believe in God, and we are living through a period when fear is the most natural of all emotions. It's paralyzing me. I cannot believe you fly off every night, out towards the French coast, knowing that there's every chance you might not make it back to base. I can't bear to believe you toss bombs out onto the dark horizon as if they were poems by Auden. Good God, Alastair, when will we be ourselves again! When will we have time to fall in love with nice young men who study engineering and wear shockingly bad suits?

I feel so lonely. Sometimes I think I'll be alone for the rest of my days, and even that seems to me to be a positive thought: Who's to say I'll have a life ahead of me and the luxury of feeling lonely? Oh God, how I hate the bloody Nazis for dragging us all so low! At night, I have terrible dreams. Angels soaring overhead. They look benign, and they're all dressed in white with huge wings—enormous feathery wings that they flap, and the sound the flapping makes is mysterious and utterly mesmerizing. But when they swoop down and brush past my hair or my shoulders, they turn into gloomy figures who want nothing more than to catch hold of me and hurl me into a bottomless hell.

It's horrible, Alastair. What's happening to us is horrible. And yet up until yesterday none of this seemed remotely possible. What on earth was it that we weren't quick enough to spot?

Am I becoming pitiful, do you think? You'd be right. It's hard not to be, all things considered. The other day, on my way to the hospital, I cut across Hyde Park. It was a magnificent day. There was a gloriously high sun overhead, so the morning had a polished, perfect stillness to it. The branches of the trees were framing the sky, and a whole patch of it was blue arabesques. I was walking along in a bit of a hurry and thinking how indifferent all that splendor was to wars and to our urge to destroy things. There was a group of soldiers next to the lake, chatting and making a lot of noise. I looked long and hard at them, one by one. They were so young; unbelievably young, I thought. One of them in particular. Dark hair, pale eyes, a look of rapt amusement that involved his whole body. The uniform hid the harmony of his physique but also showed it off. I couldn't stop myself. I walked over to them, and without a second's hesitation, I asked him, "Will you marry me?" The others burst out laughing, and I think someone whistled. The expression on the lad's face changed. Astonishment made way for something hard to describe: half anxiety, half unadulterated joy. I put my arms around his

*neck, he closed his eyes, and my tongue found its way
in between his lips. God knows how long we stood there
like that, with the people and things around us fading
to a discreet black and white to begin with, and then
melting completely away. In the end, they gave us a
round of applause. The idea of what I'd just done
made me want to laugh, but it also made me want to
weep. I heard someone say, "Hey, we're here, too! Let's
all get married!"*

*Now I can't forget the expression on that soldier's
face. I can't forget his shoulders and the way he bent
his neck, leaning down over me. It's as if he's forever
in my arms.*

*Alastair, I haven't gone mad. Believe me. I may
have spent quite a bit of time in Wales, but I haven't
lost my mind. It's just that it makes me angry to think
our youth has to end so absurdly, amid deaths and
pain and disasters everywhere. We can't let this sense
of wreckage be all we're left with. I don't want there
to come a day—if there are any days to come—when
all I have is horrid memories. You mustn't give up
hope, old boy. Keep your eyes peeled when you're in
the showers, and the first chance you get, don't stop to
think: Get cracking and make a pass at the chap you
like best. Don't think about what happens afterward.
Don't think.*

Yours forever (shamelessly),
Edna

7

North African front, August 25, 1942

    Dearest Mother and Father,
    *I am sorry not to have written lately. I feel bad
about it because I imagine you'll have been concerned,
especially Dad, who worries so much, though he doesn't
let it show and is even a little bit ashamed of it. Your
letters have reached me. I have no idea where it is I'm
writing to you from. It's complete chaos here, and these
African villages' names are so hard to pronounce that
you end up never knowing exactly where you are. The
weather has been good for the past few days, but the
heat is on its way back now, the confounded heat they
have in this part of the world. It's not like the heat we
get in the summer at home. The heat they have here is
insane, with mile after mile of scorched earth. It's like
being on another planet, a long, long way from God*

and from civilization. It's so hot that our uniforms look like rags and you end up not wanting even to wear any clothes. Who could ever have imagined I'd end up somewhere so wretched? And even their wretchedness is very different from ours—its seems to be engrained in these people's souls. I don't know if they're Christians, around here; more than anything, folk just seem half starved, to me. Folk who are half starved and can't take any more of this war. They eat these vegetables that all taste exactly the same and don't give you any sort of energy. The food disgusts me, and just lifting it to my mouth turns my stomach, so at night I often find myself dreaming about homemade fettuccine and pork chops.

In any case, I am learning to live with it, because here you have to learn to live with everything or you're asking for trouble. One of my comrades has been of great help to me. His name is Benedetto Franciosi and he's from Rome—a tall, good-looking, athletic fellow who takes pride in his uniform. He's a year older than I am. But now no one knows what's become of him, because he's been missing ever since the last skirmish we had a week ago, and we don't know if he's alive or dead. Let's hope for the best, because he was a true friend and a good medic, a generous, cheerful type whose advice has done me a power of good.

I think of you often, dearest Mother and Father. I think of all the family with love, longing to embrace you all again. There are times when I'm sorry not to have a sweetheart waiting for me and a photograph to keep me company, but in recompense there you all are, to remind me how good life is in our Italy. When I get back from the war, I think I ought to find myself a nice girl to marry and build a peaceful life with. Keep me always in your prayers. I keep you in mine. Dear Mother and Father, there are so many other things I want to tell you, but our paper is rationed and I can't rattle on. They say that in a couple of weeks there'll be an important battle. The Germans talk about it constantly. They say it's a battle that could determine our future. We're certain to win, of course, although the heat is an overriding worry. Given the state of things here, there's no fighting the heat. But we're hoping for the best and morale is high. If everything goes as it should, I ought to be getting a fairly long period of leave, and who knows, perhaps I'll come home again. I could come for the grape harvest, and it would be grand to have a drink or two with my pals. In the meantime, I hope you have news of Giuseppe. Say hello to Nina for me. It's time she got married, like we said. It would keep the family united and make life easier for all of us. Say hello to Stefano too. Say hello to everyone, no exceptions.

Your fond son,
Ernesto

Nina read the letter right away. What did he mean when he talked about her getting married, "like we said"?

What had been said? And why that odd reference to family unity and making life easier? Confusedly, Nina thought back to the confabulations that had preceded her brother's departure at the end of his last period of leave, back in January. She did remember having had the impression that many of the discussions she overheard seemed, at the time, to have to do with her personally.

The girl ran out of the house. Late morning. An October that had almost run its course. Warm, still. The sun was sitting, stubborn and indifferent, at the top of the sky. Nina felt lonely and desperate, in the middle of all that blue vastness. She wished she could run away from here and go off to war, her too, and have done with all these months of fear, and of not enough food, and of abstruse discussions. Without meaning to, she found herself heading toward Sergio's house. The young man wasn't home. No one to ask. It occurred to her that the village felt deserted. She was the only person out and about. As she approached the little piazza looking out onto the broad valley, she heard footsteps and male voices. She caught sight of Stefano Portelli with a group of other men. They were talking animatedly. As per usual—Nina thought with a prick of irritation—Stefano will be busy telling the others why this or that law or norm has to be respected if they don't want to answer for it before the courts. She loathed the sort of speeches her brother-in-law excelled at. Nina detested the law. She despised any form of generalization. She didn't give a fig about norms and codes and regulations. In fact, it seemed to her that all that hazy cerebration over concepts and abstract principles hid behind it a form of coldness, and that love (and, in its own way, religion said this too) was essentially a form of stupefaction, a happy maddening of body and soul that had nothing to do with rules or codes. And there wasn't enough of it in the world—of that madness—which was why men fought pointless wars and the Nazis had it in for the poor Jews. Sergio was against all that butchery, too. Not that he was a Communist or anything. He said he was against the business of people killing each other and dying because, like her, he saw that nothing was more important than the urgent love that grips you at certain moments, when you want to go crazy and roll around on the ground with no clothes on, and do things that are probably better left unspecified.

She made her way out of the village. On the road leading down to the Tiber she didn't encounter a soul. High overhead a fresh, silent breeze was rousing the air. Here and there it moved through the treetops, and their leaves waved like children's hands greeting a train. There was all that glory in the world, all that infinite wonder, as if to imply that war and its horrors might perhaps be nothing more than anodyne distractions. Off in the distance, she caught sight of Sergio walking across a field. He spotted her too, and they stared at each other. Nina started ducking behind the trees on the roadside, and Sergio did the same thing. They sought each other out without seeking each other, at a distance, each of them knowing the other could never be reached, because he was doomed to burn with a cold ardor that over the years would drive him into the arms of every girl in the area, while she would remain a stranger to him—the most puzzling mystery of all.

Poggio, December 5, 1942

Dear Son,
We hope this finds you alive and in good health. Here, there hasn't been much in the way of news about the war, but the other day we did hear Il Duce's speech on the radio and felt somewhat reassured. We worry about you constantly, because of the things one hears people say about the fighting with the English in Africa. Unhappily, we still have no news of your brother, Giuseppe. We continue to trust sincerely that he will come home one day, but of course our hopes do shrink a little with every day that passes. We have asked around, with the help of trusted friends, but nothing has come of it. A few of the boys who were off at the Russian front have started coming home, but so far none of them has been able to tell us anything regarding Giuseppe. But enough with these sad things. There is one piece of good news. After all your insisting, Stefano has come around to the idea, and so we have set a date for the wedding, next May. We

dearly hope you will be here too. Amid all the sadness and bad luck our family has suffered, it ought to be a moment of joy and serenity. We send you embraces and kisses, dear Ernesto, and we trust in your good judgment and in the will of the Lord.

Your loving parents

8

STEFANO PORTELLI WILL NEVER FORGET THAT KISS,
which arrives just as his desperation reaches its climax.
He will be unable to forget it because, among other
things, he will always be haunted by the idea that he
was not its real witness. More in the way of a casual
onlooker. An intruder, even—as, many years later, he
will become certain was the case: an anonymous pass-
erby who is, for a brief instant, granted the privilege of
treading the boards with the tragedy's principal players.
That is what Stefano Portelli will end up believing. And
when all is said and done, no one will be in a position
to contradict him.

There is already a whiff of change in the air. Poor Eleonora had always said as much: *Fascism will crumble
of its own accord.* To which he himself used to add:
Under the weight of its own ignominy. The atmosphere